The **WRECK**
of the **ATOCHA**

by Lisa Thompson

Copyright © 2007 Sundance/Newbridge, LLC

Published by Sundance Publishing
33 Boston Post Road West
Suite 440
Marlborough, MA 01752
800-343-8204
www.sundancepub.com

Copyright © text Lisa Thompson

First published as Treasure Trackers by
Blake Education, Locked Bag 2022, Glebe 2037, Australia
Exclusive United States Distribution: Sundance Publishing

Photography:
Cover Joel W. Rogers/Corbis

ISBN 978-1-4207-0719-9

Printed by Nordica International Ltd.
Manufactured in Guangzhou, China
March, 2014
Nordica Job#: CA21400240
Sundance/Newbridge PO#: 227672

contents

FLORIDA

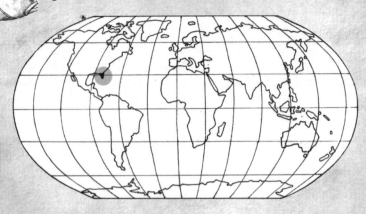

THE STORY OF NUESTRA SEÑORA DE ATOCHA

Over 380 years ago, Spanish galleons sailed the world, bringing back treasure from the many new lands Spain had colonized—especially South America.

It was dangerous work. There was bad weather, long periods at sea without nutritious food, hazardous sailing routes, and the constant threat of attack by pirates.

On September 4, 1622, a fleet of 28 ships left the Cuban port of Havana for Spain. The galleon *Nuestra Señora de Atocha* was among them. It was filled with treasure. As the fleet headed into one of the most dangerous stages of its journey—the Straits of Florida—they were hit by a hurricane. Eight ships, including the *Atocha*, sank. Only five of the 265 people on board the galleon survived.

The Spanish and many pirates made unsuccessful attempts to recover the treasure. The wreck and its cargo lay hidden for the next 350 years. In 1975, an American treasure hunter,

Mel Fisher, discovered thousands of silver coins and five coral-encrusted bronze cannons from the *Atocha*. It took another ten years before Mel and his team located the wreck and its treasure.

On July 20, 1985, Mel's son Kane radioed his father from the *Dauntless*. "Put away the charts. We've got the mother lode!" he cried.

The treasure included silver coins, more than 500 silver ingots, gold bars, gold chains, and gold plates and cups.

On May 28, 1986, recovery divers got the shock of their lives when they unearthed hundreds of shaped and uncut emeralds. One single jewel was valued at over two million dollars. It was definitely a treasure worth finding!

The Story of
Nuestra Señor de Atocha

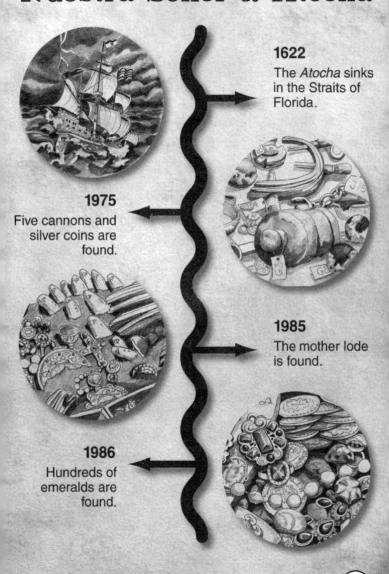

1622
The *Atocha* sinks in the Straits of Florida.

1975
Five cannons and silver coins are found.

1985
The mother lode is found.

1986
Hundreds of emeralds are found.

CHAPTER 1

Sea LEGS

"Ahoy there, Ramón! Still feeling a little green?" called Uncle Earl from the top deck of the boat. "Don't worry. We're almost at the dive site. You should have your sea legs by then."

"It's not my sea legs I'm waiting for. It's my sea

stomach," groaned Ramón as he leaned over the railing again.

"You mean your sea ears."

Ramón turned and saw his friend Mia holding out a cup for him.

"Seasickness is actually caused by an imbalance in your inner ear, Ramón. Here, take a sip of this. It'll settle your stomach."

Ramón gingerly took the cup. Everything he ate or drank sent his stomach churning.

"Mel told me to give it to you, and you know ship rules—when at sea, follow the captain's orders!"

Ramón rubbed his arm. He was still recovering from the enormous bear hug of a greeting Mel had given him. Ramón screwed up his face at the bitter taste. "Yuck! Now I really feel sick!"

"If you had worn patches, you'd feel fine. Look

at me. I feel great." Mia flashed a wide smile and held out her hand. Mia seemed to know how to prepare for any situation.

"What are Uncle Earl and Mel doing?" Ramón asked. Since boarding the boat, Ramón and Mia had hardly seen the two of them.

"Oh, they're busy talking with the crew about the wreck and looking over charts, maps, and stuff," answered Mia. "I had no idea that my uncle knew so much about Spanish shipwrecks, ocean currents, and diving."

"Yeah, your uncle's full of surprises."

This was true. When it came to things from the past, Mia's uncle was the expert's expert. He was respected around the world for his knowledge of archaeology and his wonderful discoveries. Uncle Earl was a legend, and people kept turning to him whenever they had a problem they couldn't solve.

Mel had been searching for this one wreck for years. Now, he'd finally called upon Uncle Earl to lend him a hand. The search was difficult and expensive, but Mel believed he was really onto something. Using Uncle Earl's expertise, he was sure they would find the treasure.

With only a couple of hours' notice, Mia, Ramón, and Uncle Earl had flown to Florida. After they arrived, they boarded Mel's boat, the *Dauntless*, and headed straight out to sea.

That's what life was like with Uncle Earl—short notice, exotic locations, strange problems to solve, and lots of hard work. Mia always begged for the chance to go along and, of course, her best friend, Ramón, always went along, too. Not that Uncle Earl minded the extra company!

"Two heads are better than one," he'd say. "And with three heads, we're sure to find something!"

Ramón was feeling a little better. "Hey, Mia! What's the name of the famous shipwreck we're looking for?"

"The *Atocha*. It's a Spanish galleon that was

loaded with treasure. It sank about 380 years ago. Mel's already found some of the treasure, but he can't find the hull of the ship. It's supposed to be full of gold, silver, and gemstones. He calls it the 'mother lode.'"

Mia let out a laugh. "So I guess we're sailing the high seas after the mother lode of the *Atocha*. Can you believe it!"

"Awesome!" Ramón said. "Don't say high seas, though—that makes me feel kind of queasy."

Just then Mel called to them from the ship's bridge. "Can you guys make your way to the gear deck? One of the crew will fit you out with dive suits."

CHAPTER 2

Suiting UP

"Cool!" said Mia. "Ramón, you have to check out some of the equipment on this boat." Mia loved technology. Gadgets and gizmos always impressed her. "There's some awesome stuff—high-tech gear, sonar for scanning the ocean floor, electronic chart plotters, metal detectors, and the GPS, a satellite navigation system. They've even got an ROV—that's a submarine robot with its own camera. And wait until I show you this crazy invention that Mel's come up with to help find the wreck!"

Mia led the way to the stern of the boat.

"Mia, can't it wait? Let's just try the dive gear on. Then we could drop a line over the boat to catch a fish. You know—just RELAX!"

Mia ignored him and pointed to a huge, bent, black tube. "Now, this is impressive!" she said.

Ramón narrowed his eyes. "Mia, what's so impressive about an oversized laundry chute?"

"Let me explain first!" she cried. When Mia wanted to explain something, she got very upset if you didn't let her finish. Ramón found it kind of funny. Sometimes he butted in just to annoy her.

"This oversized laundry chute is called the *mailbox*. It has already led Mel and his team to find 1,033 gold coins on the bottom of the ocean."

Ramón's eyes opened wide and his jaw dropped. "One thousand and how many?"

"I thought that would get your attention. Really cool, huh?"

"Very impressive!" said Ramón. If there was one thing Ramón loved, it was finding treasure. "So how does it work?"

"It's simple, really. It can sometimes be hard finding things on the ocean floor. What you're searching for can be buried under tons of mud and sand and stuff. So Mel anchors the boat at the site, fits the mailbox over the propellers, and turns on the engine. The gushing water from the propellers goes down the tube to the bottom of the ocean. The force of the water clears away the debris so the divers can see. Pretty good idea, isn't it?" Mia sounded so proud you'd have thought she had invented it herself.

Ramón nodded. "But can it catch fish?"

"Mia! Ramón!" Uncle Earl called. "Come on!"

They raced to the gear deck where Uncle Earl was looking over barnacle-covered items and listening to one of the crew. It was strange to see him with a frown. He was almost always in a good mood.

"Everything OK, Uncle Earl?" asked Mia as she stepped around the stack of wet suits.

"Yes. Yes. I just have a lot to do, and we don't have a lot of time. Now, do you two still want to go diving?"

"Sure!" said Ramón.

"Can't wait," said Mia.

"Good. I'll leave you with Kane. He's the dive master, so listen to what he says. Ramón, try not to touch anything, OK? This is not the place to go poking around. Mia, don't bombard Kane with too many questions. Look out, Kane. You may find Mia knows more about that ROV over there than you do!" Uncle Earl gave a chuckle. "I'll be up with Mel."

"Hey, what's this?" asked Ramón, holding up a weed and barnacle-covered shape.

"Ramón!" cried Mia. "What did Uncle Earl just say to you?"

"Well it's not like it has DON'T TOUCH written on it."

Kane came over, and Ramón handed it back. "We think it's part of one of the cannons that came off the *Atocha*. It's probably best if we don't play around with anything until Earl has had a chance to examine it." Kane started to look through a pile of wet suits. "So what size suit do you think you'll need, Ramón?"

"Medium," said Ramón, puffing out his chest. "I've been working out lately. I think I must be a medium by now."

"Yeah, right!" scoffed Mia. "Two small wet suits will be fine, thanks."

Kane handed them over. "If they don't fit, let me know." He went about gathering other equipment.

"Hey, Kane, what's wrong with Uncle Earl?" inquired Ramón as he wriggled into the black rubber suit. "He looks so serious. What's going on?"

"Oh, he's been looking through the research and charts, and he thinks we might be diving in the wrong spot. He wants us to search a new area. The trouble is, we may not have time to search both sites. The weather isn't supposed to stay good for very long. So he and Mel are trying to make the right decision."

"High seas?" asked Ramón cautiously.

"Yep. So I hope you're not someone who suffers from seasickness! It could get pretty rough out there."

Kane went through the diving gear and gave Mia and Ramón a complete rundown on all their equipment. They tested the regulators on the oxygen bottles and made some adjustments to masks, suits, and belts.

Mia tried her hardest to keep her questions to a minimum. Ramón could tell it was practically killing her. He slipped off his oxygen tank. It weighed a ton on deck, but Ramón knew that once he was in the water, he would barely feel it.

A voice came over the loudspeaker. Mel ordered everyone onto the bridge for a briefing. The boat's motor stopped, and the crew dropped anchor.

CHAPTER 3

A NEW Dive

Mia and Ramón were surprised to find out how many different skills people on board had. While almost all the crew were divers, everyone seemed to have another field of expertise as well. There were researchers, oceanographers, shipwreck specialists, artifact conservationists, salvage experts, and a medical team. It seemed that Mel was leaving nothing to chance. He wanted this team to be the best.

Mel gathered everyone around a chart of the dive area. "I think you have all met Earl, Mia, and Ramón. I asked Earl aboard to help us with our search and to work on a hunch I have.

"We're pretty short on time, so I'll be brief. Earl's examined some of the things we've found— the coins, silver bars, and cannons. He's also looked at the charts from the time when the *Atocha* went down. As a result, we've decided to dive at a new site." Mel pointed to the map. "I'll let Earl fill you in on the details."

Ramón leaned over and whispered to Mia, "With all this high-tech equipment and crew, how hard could it be to find the *Atocha?* It seems that it should be pretty easy."

"Well, it's obviously not as simple as you think, or they wouldn't need Uncle Earl. Now, shhhh. I want to hear what my uncle has to say."

Uncle Earl stood up. "As you are all aware, tides and currents can move wrecks great distances and break them up. This is why you have found pieces scattered over such a wide area. So while we do have a good idea where the ship went down, we're not certain where it lies now. After much discussion and research, I believe that the hull of the ship lies here." Uncle Earl pointed to the new site on the chart. "There's a chance of bad weather later in the day, but right now diving conditions are excellent. If it's OK with everyone, we'd like to start the search immediately. Any questions?"

Mia went to put up her hand, but Ramón grabbed it. "Let's just get in the water. Otherwise we'll be here all day!"

"I was only going to ask how long the dive would be," she said, a little embarrassed. Mia knew that Ramón was right. Sometimes she did tend to ask too many questions.

The crew got to work. All the divers were given metal detectors to take with them. The ROV was released into the water, and the sonar scanner was switched on.

Ramón and Mia struggled with their oxygen tanks. Kane came over to help them. "You two are to stay with me on this dive. Keep close and don't go wandering off. Remember to keep an eye on your tank levels."

"Don't forget the metal detectors and a lamp," Uncle Earl called.

"Today's the day!" yelled Mel. "I can just feel it. Today's the day we find the *Atocha*!"

"You say that every day!" laughed Kane as the team entered the water.

"Let's hope he's right today," said Ramón as he

fixed his mask. "I'd love to find some treasure! Come on, let's go, Mia. You don't want to be left behind for shark bait."

"What sharks? Where? No one said anything about sharks. Wait a minute. I just want to ask about something . . ."

But it was too late for Mia to back out now, sharks or not.

CHAPTER 4

An EERIE Feeling

As they descended into the water, it was eerily calm. All Ramón and Mia could hear was the hissing sound of their breathing and the release of air bubbles. Two huge manta rays and a school of fish followed them down. Slowly the sunlight through the

water began to fade, and the water turned dark
and murky.

Kane turned on his flashlight, and Ramón and
Mia turned theirs on, too. They were three little
lights swimming downward . . . downward . . .
downward . . .

Ramón and Mia had never experienced diving at
these depths. It was so still, dark, and calm that it
was scary. Here, the ocean floor was not smooth and
silty as Ramón had seen it in other places. It was a
barnacle-encrusted old reef with weed-covered rocks
jutting out.

Kane noticed something glint through the murky
waters and signaled the others to follow. He found
some Spanish silver coins, called pieces of eight,
that bore the same markings as others from the
Atocha. He gave the coins to Mia and Ramón and
then moved on.

The three traveled in single file through the old
reef. Behind each new rock, Ramón expected to see

the hull of the *Atocha*, with its vast treasure laid out before them.

The water grew darker, and it became harder for Ramón to follow Kane or his light. It was weird. Which way was up or down, right or left? For a moment, Ramón lost all sense of direction. He started to panic and breathe harder. Then he saw Mia's light above him. She was signaling for him to follow. Had she found the remains of the *Atocha* by herself?

The water felt colder as they rose. Had they drifted into a different current? Mia seemed to be leading Ramón back to the surface. They reached the top and broke through the water.

"Man . . . that was weird," gasped Ramón. "For a second I didn't know where I was. Then I saw your light."

"I got lost, too," said Mia, sounding a little panicky. "Do you have any idea where Kane went?"

Ramón didn't answer. He was staring at

something behind Mia. The sea looked the same as when they had entered the water—except that the *Dauntless* had disappeared! In its place was a 17th century pirate ship! Ramón knew it was a pirate ship because it was flying the pirate's flag—the Jolly Roger. He took off his mask to make sure he wasn't seeing things.

"Ramón!!! I'm talking to you. Did you see where Kane went?"

"What? Kane? Ummmmmm, no. Ah . . . Mia, I think you should turn around."

"This had better not be one of your stupid jokes, Ramón. We need to find Kane." She slowly turned her head. "Oh, my . . . what in the world? Ramón! That's a . . . a . . . pirate ship!"

CHAPTER 5

A Pirate SHIP?

Little Kidd raised the alarm from the crow's nest. "Captain, I see people in the water northeast of the bow."

The pirates lowered a small boat into the water and hauled Ramón and Mia aboard.

The deck of the ship was crowded with tough-looking pirates. Everyone was silent as the captain walked forward. He was the meanest-looking man Ramón and Mia had ever seen. He had weatherworn skin and several missing teeth.

"Who are you? How dare you sneak up on my ship!" he snarled. "I am Captain Bloodbath, Pirate Ruler of the High Seas. All people who sail these waters fear me. I demand to know what you are doing, or you will walk the plank." Bloodbath paused and looked at them. "What are these strange outfits you are wearing?"

Mia stepped forward. "Captain Bloodbath, nice to meet you. Thank you for saving us."

Ramón looked at Mia in disbelief. What was she doing? Bloodbath was a cold-blooded murderer, and Mia was thanking him!

Mia continued, "I've heard a lot about you. You are a great man, and I've always wanted to meet you."

"Go on," demanded the Captain.

Mia glared at Bloodbath. She SO hated being interrupted. "Well, we're pirates, too. I'm surprised you haven't heard of us! I am Mad Mia, the craziest female pirate on the high seas, and this is my good friend, Rotten Ramón."

Ramón gave his best mean and hungry scowl to the crew, though none of them seemed to notice. They were all listening to Mia.

"The ship we were on went down, and we were captured by the Spaniards. They put us in these strange suits to take us back to Spain. Once there, they were going to hang us for our pirating crimes. But we had other ideas. I was able to trick the jailer, and Ramón fought more than a dozen men before we were forced to jump overboard. Had it not been for you, we would've drowned."

"Way to go, Mia," thought Ramón. Boy, she was good at making up stuff.

Bloodbath leaned closer, so close that Mia and

Ramón drew back with small, shaky steps. "From what ship did you escape?" he growled.

Ramón had seen a ship on the horizon. "That one there, Captain Bloodbath!"

"AHHHHHH!!!!!!" hollered Bloodbath, quickly raising his sword. A hush went through his crew of scoundrels.

"Did I say something wrong?" croaked Ramón. "Maybe it wasn't that ship. Hard to tell, really. I mean you know how it is—those Spanish galleons all look the same."

"SILENCE!" yelled Bloodbath. He was now only a hair's breadth away from Ramón's face. Ramón stood in terror waiting for the strike of the sword. Then Bloodbath began to speak slowly. "You come from the *Atocha,* eh? The Spanish ship we are after? Hmm . . . how interesting. Tell me about its cargo."

"Why, it's a pirate's dream," cried Mia, diverting Bloodbath's attention. "It's packed to the rafters with gold, silver, and gemstones! The treasure on that ship will make rich pirates of us all, a thousand times over."

"All of us, hey?" He eyed her angrily with his one good eye.

"Why, of course. Spare us, and we will lead you to hidden treasures that only we know about."

The captain thought about that for a moment. With distrust in his voice he sneered, "For now, I will spare you. But be warned!" He drew his dagger, grabbed Ramón by the neck, and held the blade close to his throat. Mia gasped. Ramón could hardly breathe. The crew smiled eagerly. "I will be watching you very, very closely."

Captain Bloodbath pushed Ramón onto the deck. "Little Kidd, show our new companions around. The rest of you, get back to work. We will attack the *Atocha* tomorrow, at nightfall. I want everyone ready." He whacked the nearest pirate over the head. "Get out of my way, you idiot!" Then he stormed back to the bridge.

"That man's crazy!" said Mia. "Ramón, are you OK? You were very brave. How's your neck?"

"Oh, I'll live—for now," Ramón murmured as he looked up toward Bloodbath.

Little Kidd walked forward. "He's got a very short temper, and he didn't get his name for nothing. Here's something to wear. You'd better get out of those strange suits. Is what you say about the *Atocha* true?"

Ramón showed Little Kidd the Spanish coin Kane had given him. "There's plenty more where that came from."

Little Kidd's eyes grew wide. "I've always dreamed of such treasure. Pirates run in our family. My father was a great pirate, and I want to be one, too. Come on, I'll show you around."

CHAPTER 6

Cutthroat
CARLOS

Life aboard the pirate ship was cramped and uncomfortable. There was an endless list of jobs to do. Pirates mended sails, fixed lines, scrubbed decks, and repaired masts.

"Stay out of the way of Cutthroat Carlos. He

wants to be the next captain, and he'll hurl you overboard in a second," warned Little Kidd. "There isn't a lot of food on board—we've been at sea for a long time. Here, have a hardtack biscuit." Little Kidd flicked off the weevils. "And try a lime. I hate sucking on these things," he said wincing, "but I guess it's better than getting scurvy."

Mia took a bite of the biscuit. "Ouch!" she cried, holding her mouth. "No wonder these are called hardtacks. I think I almost broke a tooth."

Little Kidd laughed and walked to the mast. "OK, back to work," he said as he pointed skyward. "I'll do the first watch so you two can rest. Then it's your turn."

"Fine with me," Ramón replied. He was eager to get off the deck. Cutthroat Carlos looked ready for a fight, and Ramón didn't want to be his next target.

The three of them climbed up the rigging and into the crow's nest. It was a tight squeeze.

"This view is unreal," said Ramón.

"Have a look through this." Little Kidd handed Ramón a telescope. "I call it my *bring 'em near*. My father gave it to me, and he even had my initials engraved on it. See, L.K."

Ramón focused on the *Atocha*. "It's a beauty."

"Let me look," said Mia as she scanned the horizon. "There are some low clouds coming. Looks like the *Atocha's* heading into a storm."

"That it does," said Little Kidd. "That's why we'll hang back for a day and see how the galleon fares. You had best get comfortable. It can get pretty rough up here."

"Oh, no," groaned Ramón.

Ramón and Mia couldn't rest. Little Kidd's stories of pirate life had them wide-eyed with fear.

After a few hours, the wind picked up, and the waves were like mountains. The ship rolled and pitched with every wave. Ramón went from green to gray to white and then to green again as the crow's nest swung with each swell.

"I feel awful," he moaned.

The wind became stronger, and the waves grew larger. All hands were called on deck.

"Keep your eyes on that blasted boat," yelled the captain as the ship hit another wave. "If it gets out of sight, I'll make dinner out of the lot of you!"

By the middle of the night, the storm was at its peak. The ship was hitting one wave after another. The wind had turned into a howling gale. Ramón and Mia huddled low in the crow's nest. Little Kidd bravely stared out to sea while the sharp rain felt like nails piercing his skin. His *bring 'em near* never left his eye. Through it, he was the first to see disaster strike. The *Atocha* had sailed onto a reef.

"The *Atocha* has hit a reef! She's going down!" he cried. "The *Atocha* is going down!"

Ramón and Mia leaped up. Sure enough, the *Atocha* was sinking. The storm had torn its sails and rigging to shreds. Its masts were battered and broken, and the ship was being smashed violently onto the reef. The hull had been ripped open, and the *Atocha* was sinking fast. The ship's precious cargo was weighing it down.

Captain Bloodbath cursed the storm. A second later, the pirate ship took a heavy blow and was engulfed by an enormous wave. The main mast snapped, and the crow's nest crashed onto the deck below. Little Kidd, Ramón, and Mia hit the deck hard. Torn sails and rigging entangled them and everything else.

"Quick," said Mia to Ramón as they struggled to free themselves. "Let's get our wet suits!"

After they suited up, Ramón scrambled to retrieve their dive gear. It was chaos. The ship was rolling violently. The pirates were panicking. Ramón narrowly escaped a flying blade from Cutthroat Carlos. It seemed he was trying to take over the ship. He and Captain Bloodbath were locked together in a violent battle.

"Come on, you sea snake!" Bloodbath growled at

Cutthroat Carlos. "Come closer, and I'll gladly make shark bait of you!"

Mia and Ramón moved quietly to the edge of the deck as they slipped on their tanks. Within seconds, a huge wave swept them overboard.

"Hold on tight!" cried Ramón. "Whatever happens, don't let go of me."

Mia nodded. She was petrified. There was no time to think. They sank below the turmoil, down into the cold, dark sea.

The water was so churned up that it was difficult to see anything at all. Mia and Ramón had no idea which direction they were headed toward. Something bumped into Ramón's shoulder as it floated by, and he grabbed it with one hand. Frightened and freezing, Mia held on to Ramón's arm as the two swam with the fast-moving current.

CHAPTER 7

Back on BOARD

"Ramón! Ramón! Here, give him some room. He's coming to," said Uncle Earl with relief.

Ramón opened his eyes slowly and was blinded by the sun.

"Mia! Where's Mia?" he croaked.

"It's OK, Ramón. I'm right here."

"What? How?" Ramón stammered.

Mia bent down close to his ear. "Don't say a word. I'll explain later." She stroked his forehead.

"You certainly gave us quite a scare, young man," said Uncle Earl, letting out a huge sigh.

"He's OK. Probably just came up too quickly," said the ship's doctor.

"I told you to stay close to me. What happened?" asked Kane from the back.

Mel rushed forward holding a piece of timber. "Ramón, where did you get this?"

"Um . . . what is it?" asked Ramón warily.

"What is it? Why, it's a piece of the hull that we're looking for!" Mel was almost bursting with excitement. "You had it when you came up. Can you show us where it came from?"

"Well, I . . ."

Mia took over. "Of course he can. Just give him a few minutes to get it together."

"Yes, sure," said Mel. "Come on, Kane, let's turn on the mailbox and get ready for the dive." Mel rushed to the stern so fast that it looked like he might run right off the boat.

"That man's just like I am," Uncle Earl said, smiling. "He can't help it—he's always pushing himself to the limit."

"Mia, what happened?" Ramón was more than a little confused. "We hit the deck when the mast snapped, and Cutthroat Carlos was fighting with Captain Bloodbath, and the storm was horrendous, and we jumped into the water . . ."

"Shhhhhh. I'm not really sure what happened myself. But I do know that a very strong current was pulling us along when you grabbed hold of something. It was that piece of wood, and it dragged us up to the surface. When we surfaced, we were only a few yards from the *Dauntless,* and you had passed out."

"Really?"

"Yep. Mel nearly had heart failure when he saw what you had in your hand. You should have seen him jumping around. You know what else is strange? Have a look at the oxygen levels on the tanks. Ramón, we hardly used any oxygen!"

"But we were underwater for such a long time!"

"Apparently not! So, any idea where the rest of the hull is, Ramón?"

Ramón started to laugh. "Mia, don't tell me you haven't worked it out. We must be sitting right on top of it!"

Mia gasped in disbelief.

Ramón sprang to his feet, put on his gear, and dived back into the water.

"Hey! Where do you think you're going? Wait up. Wait for me," Mia called. Mia put on her gear and followed Ramón back into the water.

Kane heard the commotion and called out, "You're not going anywhere without me!" Then he dived in, too.

Mel and Uncle Earl switched off the mailbox. As the murky water cleared, they could see that hundreds of years of sand and debris had been pushed away to reveal the mother lode. The long-lost treasure of the *Atocha* had been found at last!

CHAPTER 8

The Mother LODE

Over the next week, divers worked around
the clock to bring up thousands of artifacts from
the wreck of the *Atocha.* Silver and gold coins,
rare Spanish objects, jewelry set with precious
stones, gold chains, and hundreds of emeralds were

uncovered. It was more than any of them could have ever hoped for.

It would take months and months to retrieve and catalog all the treasure from the ocean floor. Finding the priceless treasure and artifacts was only the beginning. Each one had to be recorded, studied, and restored. Mel and his team had a lot of work ahead of them.

A few days after the discovery of the mother lode, Ramón and Mia found their own diving treasure.

"Let's search away from the main site today, Mia. I say we go a little farther south. OK?"

"Sounds fine to me."

After following the reef for only a short time, they spotted something. There, lying partly covered in sand, was a gold telescope and two daggers. They picked them up and swam back to the boat.

On the side of the telescope were the letters L.K. The daggers were marked *Captain Bloodbath* and *Cutthroat C.*

Mia and Ramón were grinning and giggling as they cleaned them.

"I wonder what happened to all the pirates in the end," said Ramón.

"Who knows? Maybe they stole more treasure and lived the rest of their lives on a beautiful tropical island somewhere."

"Yeah, right! Not a ghost of a chance!" They both laughed.

Uncle Earl was eager to inspect their finds. "I wonder what the letters *L.K.* stand for? How very interesting. I'll have to look into that. And these daggers are most intriguing, too. Captain Bloodbath and Cutthroat C. They sound like two people you wouldn't want to upset! I bet these daggers have stories to tell. You two are quite a pair of pirates, with a find like this!"

Ramón and Mia gave each other knowing looks.

"Well, you just never know what you'll find on the ocean floor, do you?" said Mia.

"No, you don't," answered Uncle Earl. "You two had better hurry. I've just had another call, and we'll be leaving this afternoon."

"For where?" cried Ramón.

"What are we looking for this time?" asked Mia.

"All in good time. Just get ready. There are many treasures to be found." He laughed. "You just have to know what you're looking for."

THE END

glossary

archaeology the study of ancient people and customs

artifacts anything made by humans

bow the front end of a boat

bridge a raised deck that looks over a ship

conservationists people who protect nature or historical artifacts

crow's nest a ship's lookout at the top of the mast

current the flow of water in a certain direction

debris things left behind when something is destroyed

diverting sending on a different path

engulfed completely covered

expertise special skill or knowledge

GPS global positioning system. It allows you to find via satellite the exact coordinates of where you are, anywhere in the world.

hardtack a long-lasting biscuit eaten by sailors

horrendous worse than horrible

hull the body of a boat

intriguing interesting, curious

Jolly Roger flag flown by pirate ships

oceanographers people who study oceans

pieces of eight old Spanish coins made of
90 percent pure silver

regulators valves that help maintain a constant
flow of oxygen

ROV remotely operated vehicle

salvage save from loss or destruction

scoundrels wicked or bad people

scurvy a disease caused by a lack of vitamin C

silty feeling like very fine sand

Spanish galleon a ship used for carrying treasure
in the 16th and 17th centuries

stern the back end of a boat

more titles

Hunting Down the Grail

Quest for El Dorado

Missing Among the Pyramids

Search for the Lost Cavern

The Wreck of the Atocha

The Red Rain of Easter Island

Key of the Mayan Kingdom

Protecting the Sunken City